The

Secret

Adventure

by

Jake D'Souza

"The Secret Adventure" published through Young Author Academy.

Young Author Academy FZCO
Dubai, United Arab Emirates

www.youngauthoracademy.com

ISBN: 9798862256260

Printed by Amazon Direct Publishing.

"Imagination is more important than knowledge."

- Albert Einstein

Contents

Hello, my name is Alex and I simply love adventures. Every day, I think of finding and having new adventures.

I live in a remote village in the woods. I am the youngest child in the village, and live with my parents but I don't have any siblings.

Every day, I love going to school, where I can meet my friends and learn a lot. I think that I like adventures because a long-lost relative of ours was actually a famous explorer a long time ago, according to my family.

I decided that during one school holidays I would set myself a challenge for ten days, I would keep myself busy with filling my days with new adventures; some small adventures and some new and interesting ones.

I would write all the adventures down in my new book, I got for my birthday just to remember all the exciting and memorable times I have experienced.

- Chapter One -

Seeking Adventures

DAY ONE

Adventure # 1 – 'Spider is Home'

On the first day of my adventure, I went to find a spider. I was always desperate for a pet, but I didn't know which one to get. I walked through the village in search of a spot where a spider could be. I searched for hours, and there behind a house in the dirt, was a spider, just sitting there on the house wall. I put the spider in a jar and claimed my very first pet. I named him Spike.

I put Spike on my bedside table so that I could see him any time I wanted to; when I wake up and when I go to bed.

I showed my mother the spider but she begged me to take it outside. I took Spikey outside and kept him in a larger terrarium in our shed, in the backyard.

DAY TWO

Adventure # 2 – 'Hide 'N Seek'

On the second day of my adventure, I woke up early and went to play hide and seek with some of the other children living in the village.

Our village was small with only about fifty people living there. Many different kinds of people lived in our village; strict and serious people, funny people and more, but mainly merchants. The most popular job in the town was being a merchant. There was a store where the village people could buy their groceries, a very small school with teachers who would teach the children, and other people who would help their fellow villagers with building houses and keeping their village tidy.

I would often hide outside, near the corner of a house in the village. It had some great hiding holes, which is why it is was my favorite hiding spot. The house was next to the nearby forest.

On this particular day when I was hiding from my friends, I noticed some large apple trees which I wanted to come back to later. The apples looked delicious and so scrumptious that I wanted to take a bite of the juicy apple.

Even though I played with some of the other children in the village, I was really lonely, but on this second day of my adventure, I met a new friend.

In looking for another hiding spot, I was jogging along in the village when I saw a boy who appeared to be drowning in the river. His arms were flailing all over the place and he was yelling out 'help'. I helped him by pulling him out of the water, and that's how I made my first ever best friend. The boy's name was Liam. We went back to the village and he went back to his family. I told him about my adventures and he was very happy to join me on my adventures as a sidekick. _

DAY THREE

Adventure # 3 – 'A New Friend'

On the third day of my Ten Day Adventure Challenge, after quite an adventurous first couple of days, I went and met my new friend, Liam, at his house and we went to pick some apples from the trees nearby. I loved apples, they are my favourite food. We went to the apple orchard in our village and spent the afternoon picking apples.

DAY FOUR

Adventure # 4 – 'The Treasure Hunt'

On the fourth day, I decided that because I loved treasure hunts so much, I would look for an adventure to have, with the plan to go and find some hidden treasure. Liam set me up on a treasure hunt, he spent the morning creating an awesome map.

There was no prize money to be found, it was just for fun, but I was devastated when I couldn't find anything and Liam was gone and had fallen asleep by the time I had finished the treasure hunt.

I had taken too long to look around the village in search of something, but I hadn't checked the one and only place that I should have looked... the place that was marked with an X, so I immediately found my way to the x mark and started to dig!!!

I dug and dug and dug! But I only found a piece of paper, which read...

Dear Reader,

The treasure that has not been found in the past hundreds of thousands of years has been really popular in the past two weeks and I have found the one and only piece of treasure, so I am asking you to claim your reward. It's your choice. Good luck !)

Of course, it was all for fun and set up by Liam. We had a really fun day of treasure hunting adventures. But I didn't know what was about to happen in real life.

DAY FIVE

Adventure # 5 – 'A New Group'

On the fifth day, Liam and I went to make some new friends in the village. We loved playing games and going on adventures, so we thought it would be a great idea to find some other friends to play with us.

It didn't take us long to find some friends because it turned out there were a few kids playing in the middle of the village where the main fountain was.

The plan was really simple; we just had to ask if we could play, and BOOM! That was it, we suddenly had new friends. We loved to play tag or hide-and-seek but most of all, we loved to play football.

DAY SIX

Adventure # 6 - 'Space Trip'

On the sixth day of my adventures, Liam and I pretended to go to space. We loved learning about space and loved creating and building makeshift structures, so we decided on the sixth day, that we would build ourselves a pretend spacecraft.

We cut out a space-pod for Liam and myself to go on this marvellous mission!!! He tried to make the space mission realistic by using some extra details and features like larger boosters and extra engines.

We spent all day building and playing with cardboard boxes that turned into spacecraft and we pretended that it took us to space. When it started to become late, Liam went home to his place, and said he would be back the next day.

DAY SEVEN

Adventure # 7 – 'A Project of Dreams'

On the seventh day, Liam and I came over from his place and we continued redesigning our 'pretend rocket' and playing our space mission games. We continued to change the design of our crafts to make our play more interesting.

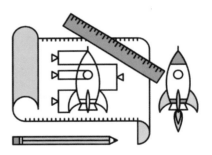

DAY EIGHT

Adventure # 8 – 'A Mysterious Letter'

On the eighth day, I rested at home, having kept busy from the space mission fun that Liam and I were having.

Later in the evening, I happened to pick up a newspaper that mum had left on the kitchen table, when I saw an article that read,

DAILY NEWS
Word • Business • Finance • Lifestyle • Travel • Sport • Weather

"Fifty three years ago, an explorer learnt about a precious undiscovered crystal, when he stumbled across it whilst exploring some ancient land."

The article continued,

The brave and humble local man was exploring the remote jungle one day in search of any interesting new finds, when he came across a large, shiny crystal. He decided to return to the village without taking the crystal from its place . He chose not to take the crystal because he did not want to remove it from its location, as he was scared. He thought perhaps something bad would happen; the ground would shake or something dangerous, or even something magical could happen, for he knew that it was not his to take.

The explorer returned to his village without the crystal and told his fellow village friends what he had found, and also why he chose not to bring it back.

Over time, other villagers went in search of this crystal but never found it. Even more mysterious, they never returned, they were forever missing..

No one has returned ever since.

Over the next few years will the crystal be found? Will people claim what they think they deserve? Will nature hand over to humanity this mysterious crystal? Only time will tell !

This is a story that may live forever and maybe we will never be able to find or describe the magical, mythical item.

So the big question is, will this crystal ever be discovered? Or will it remain in the forest for the coming centuries?

There's only one way to find out!

by John Smith,
Journalist and Reporter.
The Village Daily News

I finished reading the article and I was filled with excitement. Not only about the article, but I now had a new adventure, a real life adventure for Liam and I to go on, an adventure to find the precious crystal. I had a strong feeling that I could do it, find the crystal and bring it home. I went to bed and thought hard about what I needed to do to prepare for our big adventure.

DAY NINE

Adventure # 9 – 'Almost Here'

Liam and I spent the ninth day of our Ten Day of Adventures gathering some supplies. I even invited some of my friends in the village to join us on our brave mission!

But what I didn't count on was, when I was looking in our attic for camping and adventure supplies, I looked inside a box that belonged to my mum, and lo and behold, I found an old map, wrinkled and old, and a

little torn around the edges. This was not just an ordinary map, it was a map of the forest. And furthermore, it had a mysterious x marking on it, deep in the forest as well as many markings on the map, which I believed to be hints of how to go through obstacles and challenges.

What was she doing with a map of the forest? Maybe everyone in the village had their own map.

I slipped it into my rucksack and hoped that it would help us find our way through our adventure.

- Chapter Two -

Crystal Clear Mission

DAY TEN

Adventure # 10 – 'The Big Day'

Finally, on the tenth day, I was ready to finish my Ten Day of Adventures, and we set off on our mission to the jungle.

I went knocking on the doors of my friends throughout the jungle, and handed out the supplies. We rechecked our packing list and gathered everything together. Then we set off!

Packing List

Food
Water
Shelter
Insect repellent spray
Sleeping Bags
Climbing Ropes Equipment
Hiking Boots

We had been creeping through the jungle for an hour when from the corner of my eye, I saw monkeys swinging from branch to branch whilst toucans soared through the sky.

After walking for a little longer, we came across something interesting, the Temple of Space. We discovered it fairly easy, we were exploring through our jungle adventure and we found the vine-covered temple.

The Temple of Space was a natural structure, we had heard all about this special place in school. You could tell it was ancient, apparently it had been around for a few centuries. Its nickname was 'The Ancient Structure'.

Stories tell that when you go inside, there is a security system which has a password but we didn't have this information as it had been there for a long time and no one had ever maintained it. We tried to enter the beautiful structure, but there was no way of getting inside.

Then I remembered the map that I found in our attic. I opened up my rucksack and took out the map. I knew how to get there manually but I did use the map just incase we got lost.

We walked further into the forest, and came to realize that this would be much harder than we ever expected. Liam and I studied the map for any landmarks or things along the way.

According to my new map and the newspaper article combined, we knew that there would be mazes, spikes, hacking systems and so much more, this would not be easy. We were determined to find this unexpected magical mythical crystal.

- Chapter Three -

The Obstacles

After leaving the ancient temple, we continued on walking through the forest. According to the map, there were a series of obstacles that we had to choose one of to pass to reach the next set of obstacles.

The first obstacle was a maze. We all thought this would be easy, as we all loved mazes, so we considered this challenge.

The second obstacle was a large pond filled with freezing cold ice cubes.

The third was a deep deep hole, when they said deep, they meant deep. Our challenge was to somehow reach the other side.

The fourth route had nothing, well nothing but dirt, dirt and more dirt.

And finally, the last obstacle one had air, I mean it was full of nothing except one bottomless hole leading to a void. So the question was, which route would be the safest?

We decided to take route two; the large pond filled with ice cubes. It didn't seem so dangerous, only uncomfortable.

After leaving the first obstacle route, the next obstacle in our way was a hacking challenge. While nothing was on the map to let us know that there was a hacking challenge ahead, we came to a sign with a figure of a hacker.

Of course I didn't know how to hack but a few others in our group of friends who were with me did, so they started this challenge while I helped other people complete the first level of challenges.

The order was simple, well it was not that simple, first we needed to log in to the system on the door that was in front of us, to actually hack it, in order to enter it to reach the next set of obstacles. Secondly, we needed to possess a special material to hack the door.

To finally complete the challenge, we then needed to complete a formula to get the door open. Luckily, we all had the skills to complete the challenge. As all of my crew had passed through the door, and were waiting for the rest of the group to reach the hacking challenge, they took a bit of a power nap to boost their energy a little.

Afterwards, the map led us to a spike wall. Our challenge was to climb some spikes without falling. I knew it was going to be difficult, and I initially felt that I couldn't do it, but I tried anyway. I climbed as fast as I could but some members of our group people didn't make it and were left behind.

I made it.

There were still some friends who did make it with me, but I needed to leave them behind. I knew they would be safe. We all had four more obstacles to go, according to the map.

Now at last... it was time to get that crystal!

It was getting dark so we all rested and looked forward to the final obstacles until that crystal was ours. So far, we had finished a few obstacles, choosing a route and hacking to enter through the secret door.

After a nights sleep, we all woke up refreshed, with excitement and energy because it was our last day on our jungle adventure. With no obstacles to complete, according to the map, we continued our mission to find the crystal.

We decided to take a rest but suddenly, a voice came from nowhere, literally like it was booming all around us. It sounded just like my father's voice, but different. I felt like I had heard this voice before, if only there was a clue.

I gave it a lot of thought and thought and thought, until suddenly...

The voice boomed again....

"Hello my dear players, I hope you are fine. You are close to the crystal. You've come very far but I am warning you... you need to step up your game because the challenge is about to become more difficult."

We soon learned from the voice that our next challenge was to find five books. The number on each book was to share its order in the series.

I was frozen in fear, and so was my crew. They didn't know what to do, it was just crazy.

We still wondered what and where the voice came from? Was it all just a big game?

Then I realized we just needed to find the five books, as instructed by the voice and the map; we since found a minuscule marking on the map that showed our approximate location with a picture of five books. We had never seen it before.

We split into groups with the remaining crew members, with two people in each group. I was in Group One with Liam.

Group One would find two books. Group Two would find one of the books, Group Three would need to find one book and Group Four would also need to find one book.

We all spent the rest of the day scurrying around the forest, looking for hidden books. We were successful in that we found the books that we needed to. Finding the books wasn't a huge challenge, but we did need to look for a long time.

Afterwards, everyone got in their sleeping bags and tucked up for a good night's rest. What would await their dreams?

The Next Day...

We were startled with the noises of rustling of the trees around us. Suddenly, there was a strange but familiar looking man approaching our campsite.

He was an old man, but he looked very familiar. Suddenly, I realised that he looked like the explorer from the news article, just older.

He spoke, "Congratulations on making it this far. You must be exhausted from all the obstacles, so, if you complete this course, you will be rewarded with the crystal... So what are you waiting for?

... GO !!"

Excitedly, without stopping to ask questions, one by one, we went from jumping pillars to dodging crazy spikes. Only two of us made it through the obstacles, Liam and myself.

After completing the final challenges, the explorer emerged from the forest shrubbery again. Ready to hand over the crystal, he announced his identity...

"Alex, I am your long-lost grandfather. I have not been in your life for a while now, as I have been searching for many artefacts for many years all around the world.

But I promise you, I will be involved in your life from now on, because my duty has been fulfilled. You are quite the explorer and adventurer, yourself. Congratulations on your curiosity and your strength in making it through the obstacles. I set up all of this adventure-filled set of challenges here in this forest for you and your friends. I wanted to make sure that you were worthy of the special crystal that I found a long time ago. I am proud of you. Now, let's go home and celebrate your adventure."

After getting over the shock of my long-lost grandfather appearing in front of us, Liam and I followed him back to the village, feeling shocked but so happy. My grandfather was none other than the famous explorer. I couldn't believe it.

My parents reunited with my grandfather, and from that day on, we had the most amazing adventures together.

But you ask, what powers did the crystal possess in the end?

My grandfather revealed to me that the crystal itself, did not possess any powers at all. He revealed that the crystal was a symbol of our own strength and curiosity; that was the magic, he said. I passed the test and that's all that mattered, so he said.

About the Author

Jake D'Souza

Jake D'Souza started his writing journey at the age of seven. Born and raised in Dubai, Jake's passion for storytelling was ignited by his love for reading. He dreams of becoming an author of a best-selling novel, weaving tales that will leave an indelible mark on the hearts and minds of his readers.

Jake is also a conscious environmentalist, driven by a strong sense of responsibility towards the planet. Jake actively participates in his school's "eco warrior" team, working alongside fellow students to promote sustainability and raise awareness about environmental issues. In his spare time, Jake loves to play football and play lots of games with his new pup "Cooper".

To follow Jake's publishing journey, please visit,

www.youngauthoracademy.com/jake

[Scan Me

with your device]

Printed in Great Britain
by Amazon